HOLLY KELLER

Geraldine's Blanket

MULBERRY BOOKS • New York

Greenwillow Books, a division of
William Morrow & Company, Inc.,
1350 Avenue of the Americas,
New York, NY 10019.
Printed in the
United States of America
First Mulberry Edition, 1988

10 9 8 7 6 5 4 3 2

Library of Congress
Cataloging in Publication Data

Keller, Holly.
Geraldine's blanket.

Summary: When her mother and
father insist that Geraldine
get rid of her baby blanket,
she finds a new way to keep it
with her all the time.
[I. Blankets—Fiction] 1. Title.
PZ7.K28132Ge 1984   [E]   83-14062
ISBN 0-688-07810-9

FOR MY MOTHER

Geraldine had a pink blanket.

Aunt Bessie sent it when Geraldine
was a little baby.

And Mama put it in her crib.

Even when she got bigger,
Geraldine loved her blanket.

She took it with her everywhere.

"You won't need your blanket at the market,"
  Mama said.
"I will," Geraldine insisted.

And she always found a use for it.

When the blanket got dirty,
Geraldine helped wash it.

When there were holes,
Mama covered them with patches.

And when the edges were all frayed,
Mama trimmed them.

But Geraldine only loved it more.

"There's hardly any blanket left," Papa said.
He was getting cross.

Geraldine covered her ears.

"It looks silly," Mama said.

"Then don't look at me," Geraldine said,
    stamping her foot.

Mama tried to hide the blanket in the closet.

But Geraldine found it right away.

She kept it pinned to her dress all day.

And tucked it under her pillow at night.

Mama and Papa talked in whispers.

And at Christmas there was a new present from Aunt Bessie.

The doll's name was Rosa,
and Geraldine loved her.
"But I still want my blanket," she said.

"No," Papa said.
"No," Mama agreed.

Geraldine knew what to do.

"There," she said when she had finished.
"Now Rosa has the blanket and I have Rosa."

Mama didn't know what to say.
Papa scratched his head.

And Geraldine took Rosa out to play.